A BAD YEAR FOR DRAGONS

The Legend of Saint George

Retold and drawn by JOHN RYAN *

The Bodley Head
LONDON

The story goes that once, long ago, there lived a young soldier called George. He was brave and strong and good, but, unlike many people in those far-off days, George was also a Christian.

He had a sword which looked like a cross.

"One day," he said to himself, "when I meet something really wicked, I will use it as both a sword and a cross."

And with this thought George set out on his adventures.

Now it happened to be a particularly bad year for dragons. Some flew in the sky, so huge and violent that they destroyed buildings with their flapping wings and flailing tails.

Some swam in the ocean. They made the water boil and many ships and sailors were lost.

There was little George could do about them: he couldn't fly, and he was no sailor.

Then George heard about another dragon, this time on land, and the most terrible of them all.

It had made its home in a great marshy swamp near a city called Sylene, and it sounded very wicked indeed.

"Now that one I *could* deal with," thought George, and he set off to find it.

The dragon of Sylene certainly was a terrible beast. When it had first arrived, the people of the city tried to kill it or drive it away. But one blast of its poisonous fiery breath put them to flight. Some couldn't run fast enough . . .

and the dragon gobbled them up.

After that, the people put out two sheep every day for the dragon to eat, and for a time all was peaceful again. But then the dragon got bored with eating sheep, and decided that it would really like to eat people—nice, tender, *young* people.

When he heard about this, the King of Sylene called his citizens together and said,

"There is only one way to manage this dreadful affair: we must draw lots. Every morning all our young people must pick a pebble out of a sack. One of the pebbles will be white, the rest black. Whoever picks the white pebble will be the dragon's dinner that day."

So, next morning, all the youths and maidens gathered together in the market place. Each took a pebble from the sack . . .

and held it, hand clenched, so that no one else could see the colour.

When everyone had a pebble, the order was given to look at them. For a moment nobody moved.

Then, one after another, they held up their pebbles.

There was a sudden cry. It came from the King's only daughter, the Princess Sabra.

She had picked the white pebble!

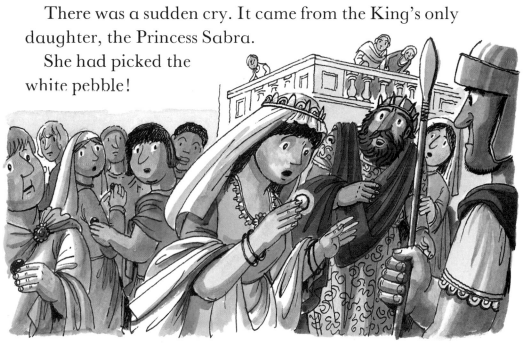

The King was horrified.
"This is impossible!" he
cried, and he offered all the
gold and silver he had if the
people would send someone
else to the dragon. But the
crowd would have none of it.

"Come now, that's not fair!"
they shouted. "You made the
law—now you must keep it."

The King saw that he was beaten. He had always hoped to
see his daughter married in great splendour, but now he knew
this could never be.

So, when the time came for Sabra to be taken to the dragon,
he had her dressed as a bride, in a beautiful wedding gown,
with flowers in her hair,
and a bouquet
in her hand.

Then the King kissed his daughter good-bye, and she was led
out to the edge of the marsh.

There she was left
all alone and very
frightened.

At that moment George came riding by on his way to
the city.

"Who are you?" he asked, "and why are you sitting out
here on your own?"

So the Princess told him all about the dreadful dragon, and
how she had drawn the white pebble. "And now," she ended,
"you had better escape yourself before the monster arrives.
There is nothing you can do for me!"

"Well!" said George. "We'll see about that."

From the walls of Sylene the crowd were watching. They saw the young horseman arrive and wondered who he was.

Then they saw something else . . .

The dragon was rising from the swamp.

Shaking the mud from its
scaly body, and breathing
poisonous fumes from its
nostrils, the terrible dragon
advanced on the Princess.

"Run!" cried Sabra,
but George paid no attention. Raising his sword, he held it like
a cross before the dragon.

At that, the terrible flaming breath died away, and George was able to get close to the dragon. Wheeling his horse, he charged . . .

and a fearful battle began.

The dragon snapped its huge jaws and thrashed its spiky
tail, lashing out with its cruel claws as George attacked,

and the Princess cheered him on.

At last George struck the beast such a fierce blow

that it gave one final roar of fury and sank to the ground exhausted.

"There!" cried George, turning to the Princess.

"Lend me your sash."

So Sabra untied the sash and gave it to him.

George slipped one end of the sash round the dragon's neck, gave the other end to Sabra, and asked her to lead the dragon into the city. It was a strange sight. First came George with his horse, then the Princess leading the dragon. The great beast had become strangely meek and tame, yet when the people saw what was coming they fled in terror.

But George called to them, saying, "It's all right! You have nothing to fear now."

Then the King came forward and hugged his daughter
and clasped George by the hand.

"How is it, young man," he asked, "that you can defeat our
terrible enemy, when
we have all failed?"

"Ah, well," said
George. "I am a
Christian, and
my sword is like
Christ's cross.
That is stronger
than any evil
anywhere."

"So you have shown me," said the King, "and I must now believe in the power of your God. We had better all become Christians too!"

Everyone rejoiced that the dragon was beaten. The King gave a splendid party which went on all night, and the next morning the people of Sylene became Christians.

There are different stories about what happened after that. Some say that George married the Princess Sabra and they lived happily ever after. Others say that George went on to have many more adventures, but was finally martyred for his Christian belief.

And what happened to the dragon? Some stories say that George killed it by cutting off its head. But that does seem rather hard, since it had now become so gentle.

Perhaps the dragon stayed in Sylene, helping to carry heavy loads,

and to protect the city from invaders . . .

and maybe it kept the children out of mischief, too

British Library Cataloguing in Publication Data
Ryan, John, *1921–*
A bad year for dragons: the legend of Saint George.
I.   Title
823'.914 [J] PZ7
ISBN 0–370–31005–5

Printed in Great Britain for
The Bodley Head Ltd, 32 Bedford Square, London WC1B 3EL
by William Clowes Ltd, Beccles
First published 1986

George was later called 'Saint' George, because of the good things he had done during his life, and because of the strength of his Christian faith.

English soldiers in the Crusades believed they saw George fighting on their side, so he has become the patron saint of England.

Saint George's day is celebrated on 23 April each year.